GIBSON

A MONEY, POWER & SEX SHORT STORY

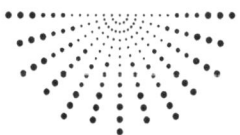

NORIAN LOVE

Copyright

ISBN-13: 978-1-7366707-7-4

ISBN-10: 1-7366707-7-8

© 2023 by Norian Love

© 2023 by Project 7even Publishing

For my Family
Country Above Self

1

FRESHMAN YEAR

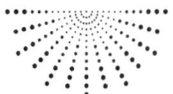

*S*tupid, lazy girl! I have no patience for this rubbish. Answer your phone or be ready to pack your bags to leave on Sunday!

Shanice Gibson ignored the text from her aunt Theresa. For the last month she'd been looking for a job, but her aunt lived in a rural area, so opportunities were limited, especially for her. By the time each school year started, all the kids at Robert Lee High School had taken whatever was available. Being a transfer, chances were slim-to-none of finding an after-school job.

"I'm not dealing with this right now. As soon as she hears about the fight, I'm gone, anyway," she muttered to herself.

A part of her missed Nevis, the small Caribbean island she'd lived on her whole life, but going back meant the end of her dream.

Where are you? Pick up the phone!

She ignored her aunt again. She figured she could at least have one day to herself without being screamed at every night.

As she walked, she looked around and took in the changing leaves as they fell indiscriminately from their branches. The weather was starting to cool, and she had only a light sweater on – this may be the last good day to do something she'd wanted to do since she'd arrived in the country.

"You know what? I'm gonna have a snow cone," she said aloud, her spirits lifting.

Wintertime Snow was the local hangout near the high school. She'd heard so much about the snow cone store from the other kids, but had never had the opportunity to go, since she was too busy with her schoolwork or the endless list of chores her aunt had for her.

As she walked in, the checkered blue-and-white floor and the soft sky-blue walls gave her a sense of calm. For the first time since she'd arrived in America, she relaxed.

"You know, that's why we did it, right?" a familiar voice startled her.

She'd hoped to see him here.

Without turning around, she said, "Did what, exactly?"

"Paint the walls that color. You were relaxing, right?"

"How did you—"

"I saw it when you walked in. You looked like you had the weight of the world on your shoulders, and then the moment you walked in, you glanced around and almost cracked a smile."

This time she did smile.

She looked at the brown-skinned boy she'd been crushing on since she got to school as he extended his hand.

"Hi, I'm Marcus, Marcus Winters."

"Shanice Gibson. Nice to meet you."

"Gibson? Do I kn—"

"So, your family owns this place?" Shanice cut him off.

Marcus let it slide. "Yeah, they own it, but I do all the work. My dad says every man needs to understand what it takes to build something, so I do all the ordering, all the painting, and all the cleaning, while he gets all the money."

The two chuckled.

Shanice wasn't sure what to say next, but she knew she didn't want the conversation to end. "Sounds like my aunt. She wants me to find a job and basically turn my money over to her."

"That's crazy, you know what I mean? I spent the entire summer making sure this place was dope, you know – the paint, the light fixtures – and everything but the bare minimum came out of my pocket so an adult could make retirement."

Shanice walked over to one painting, a life-sized portrait of a rapper wearing a white Adidas sweatsuit, a big gold chain, and a Kangol hat, standing next to an 80s boombox.

"That's a sick picture of LL Cool J. Did you paint that?" she asked.

Marcus walked over to her and nodded. "I did, but… it's supposed to Jay-Z."

Shanice bit the inside of her cheek to suppress her chuckle.

Picking up on this, Marcus replied, "It's okay, I know it's not that good."

"No, it's actually an amazing mural of LL."

Marcus dropped his face into his hands in embarrassment.

"But in your defense, a lot of people don't know Jay Z used to dress like this back in the day." Shanice released the chuckle she'd been holding in.

"Wait, a second. Gibson… Gibson… don't we take biology together?"

Her apprehension returned with his question. "Um, we do, but—"

"You're the girl that everyone is texting about, the girl that punched Trina Carter in the face after school today, aren't you? You're Right Hook!"

"That's not my name."

"I'm sorry, but the way you whooped Trina's ass today, that's what everyone's gonna be calling you tomorrow."

Shanice smiled. If there was a silver lining to the day, it was being able to punch Trina in the face. Still, she knew as soon as her aunt found out, her life would effectively be over.

"Well, I won't be there tomorrow or any other day, because as soon as my aunt finds out I'm suspended, she's gonna put me back on a boat to Nevis and I'm gonna have to work in the hotel industry for the rest of my life."

"Nevis? I've heard of that. About two hours south of Puerto Rico, right?"

His words stunned her. It was the first time since she'd been in the U.S. that someone had heard of her homeland.

"That's right! How did you...?"

"My dad is in the military and quizzes me on geography all the time. Domestic and international. For instance, did you know there was a place called Cut and Shoot, Texas? Not sure if I'd want to live in a place called Cut and Shoot. Especially with our complexion."

Shanice laughed at the implied joke as Marcus continued. "Oh, so you really are fresh off the—an island girl," he quickly corrected, catching himself on the insult that got Trina punched in the face.

Shanice nodded and replied. "Born and raised, well technically, I was born in the states but we moved home before I was two years old, and after today I'll be going back, no question. I just came in here because I've never had an American snow cone before, and I wanted to try one."

Marcus looked at her, confused. "Wait a second, you've never had a snow cone before?"

"I mean, we had kool cups where I'm from, but not really a snow cone."

"You're in for a treat. I don't do a lot of things right, but I can make a mean snow cone," he promised as he ushered her into one of the open red booths. "Have a seat. Let's get you squared away. First, let me see the paperwork they gave you after the fight."

Shanice dug into her bag and pulled it out.

Marcus examined it like a lawyer reviewing a death row case. After a spell, he said, "So, technically the fight happened after school, and it's an unspoken policy at Lee High that they only contact your parents if it happened during school hours. So, all you really have to do is sign this form and turn it back in, and she'll never know. What's your aunt's name?"

"Theresa, but—"

Marcus pulled a pen out of his pocket and signed on the line asking for a parent or guardian signature. When he was finished, he handed the form back to Shanice and said, "Turn this back in tomorrow and serve your time. They'll never call her. Trust me on this."

"Sounds like you have some experience with this."

"I fractured a law or two in the first semester. Now, I'm gonna get you a snow cone, on the house."

"No, you don't have to—"

"Trust me, everything around here is on me. It's the least I can do, but you gotta let me choose the flavors."

"Okay, but I owe you one," she conceded, stunned by his confident nature, her dark skin hiding the fact she was blushing. It was certainly the nicest thing anyone had done for her this week.

Since the first day of school, Trina Carter had been calling her 'fresh off the boat', and it was bothering her. To make matters worse, the nickname was catching on. It all came to a head today during last period when Trina caught her staring at Marcus and poked fun at her. Shanice finally exploded, punching Trina in the face, knocking her down instantly. By playground rules, she'd won the fight, but in reality, she'd lost the war. The assistant principal wrote them both up.

As Marcus arranged the flavors, he yelled over the snow cone machine. "Yeah, Principal Allen never remembers anything. Serve your time and be out. Only thing is, try not to fight while you're in there, because I'm sure Trina is gonna be in there with you."

"Ugh! I hate that girl. She's so annoying,"

"She wasn't like that in middle school. She was a big health geek, but now she's trying to fit in with the would-be hood rats of the school. What were you two fighting about, anyway?"

"Well, you know how she is," Shanice said nervously. It was embarrassing enough to know that the fight was over a boy. There was no way she could ever tell him the fight was about *him*.

As Marcus continued to make the snow cone, Shanice smiled. It was the first time since she'd been in the country that she felt comfortable talking to anyone, and it was the person she most wanted to talk to. The butterflies in her stomach were fluttering, and she loved every moment.

Her blissful daydreaming was interrupted by a hard thud across the back of her head. Shanice suspected it was Trina coming in to get revenge.

She stood up and turned around, raising her clenched fist to swing, when she stopped in her tracks.

It was her Aunt Theresa.

"So, this is what you do with your time, hmm?" the woman scolded.

"I—"

"I nah wan' hear it! Get your things."

Shanice was about to gather her things when she heard Marcus addressing her aunt.

"Excuse me, miss, my family owns this establishment and I'm the manager, and I have to say, I don't appreciate how you're speaking to my employee."

Shanice held her breath and watched as Theresa turned to address him, surprised by what she'd just heard.

"Excuse me. De girl work for you?"

"Today was her first day, and so far, she's been phenomenal until this unpleasantness. Shanice, is this customer giving you a hard time?"

Marcus's direct nature caught her off guard. She knew her aunt was humiliated. As a hard-working, West Indian woman, embarrassing anyone at their job was a cardinal sin.

She looked at her aunt and then back to Marcus. "I'm fine, Mr. Winters, this is—"

"I'm a customer," Theresa interjected. "And me... excuse me, I'm sorry, my accent is rough, so it may be loud. I wasn't fussing at the girl. We talk a little more harshly to each other in our culture." Her aunt looked at her and said, "I'm sorry to have interrupted your work. I have to leave now."

"You don't want a snow cone?" Marcus said, still selling the bit.

"No, thank you, I must be going. I'll let you both get back to work."

Shanice watched her aunt, now ashamed, walk out of the store.

She heaved a giant sigh. Her anxiousness was gone for now. She turned towards Marcus. "Thank you. You didn't have to do that."

He shrugged his shoulders and sat across from her in the booth. "Like I said, I know what overbearing parents are like."

"It's unbearable. It's already tough not knowing anyone here, but to come home to that? You know what? It doesn't matter. As soon as she realizes I don't have a job, I'm on the first boat back home. Unless I find an actual job between now and—"

"What are you talking about? You got an actual job."

The words startled Shanice.

"You just said you owe me one, and since I pay for everything around here anyway, I'll pay you out of my check."

"Wait, are you serious?"

"Dead serious. Gives me time to make my murals look like the people they're supposed to look like. In fact, your first assignment is to try this snow cone."

Shanice smiled at the boy who handed her the snow cone. As she tasted it, her eyes lit up. "This is amazing!"

"I knew you'd like it!" Marcus said, banging the table, proud of his work.

Shanice continued to eat the snow cone. "What's in it?"

"I put in blue bubblegum, sour green apple, and sour cherry. I call it my ocean water surprise!"

PRESENT DAY.

"JUST BREATHE, lady, you ingested lots of ocean water. I'm surprised you're still with us. Just breathe."

Shanice struggled to open her eyes. Her entire body ached in indescribable ways. Her breathing was shallow, and she felt like she was suffocating.

"Cough it up, lady, you can do this."

The man pressed heavily on her chest.

She turned and coughed violently, spewing what felt like liters of ocean water into a nearby bucket.

Her breathing stabilized, but her throat still burned, and she was exhausted. She tried to stay awake, but it was hard.

She wasn't sure where she was or what had happened, but her immediate concern was why she was handcuffed to the bedpost rail.

2

SOPHOMORE YEAR

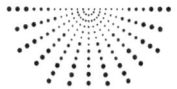

"*T*rina, hurry up, you know I got work in two hours!" Shanice was yelling at her best friend, Katrina Carter, who was still sitting in the car, putting on her makeup outside the back-to-school party hosted at Wintertime Snow.

"The lies we tell ourselves. You just want to look in that boy's face and hope that if you stare at him long enough, he'll fall in love with you."

"What? No, I'm so over Marcus. We're just good friends. Besides, he helped me out when I first got here. The least I can do is show him some support."

"The least you could do is quit playing like you don't get jealous every time he's with Bianca Torres. I see the way you look at him, Shan Shan. I don't know why you didn't just stay at that dusty ass snow cone shop, anyway."

"Because this job pays more money, and I get more freedom to do stuff like drop you off at parties."

"Oh, so you took this job for me? Because I thought it was all the free oil changes and car maintenance your auntie gets out of the deal."

"It definitely keeps her off my ass. But I enjoy working on cars. I like working with metal."

"Girl, what you need to do is stop trying to work with metal and learn how to work with wood. And by wood, I mean di—"

"I know what you mean, Trina. Hell, it's all you ever talk about. Which is strange because I'm pretty sure you haven't gotten any yourself."

Trina rolled her eyes, then shrugged. "Look, I'm keeping my legs closed because I have goals. But you better believe I will leave this Earth unchaste. You, on the other hand, have decided that you want to get shot at for the rest of your life, so you might as well get some pipe before you catch a bullet. But I'm not gonna say anything else about it. Hell, that's how I got my ass beat last year."

"Served you right, you know you were out of pocket."

"Believe it or not, I was trying to help."

Shanice pulled the car over and looked at her friend in disbelief. "Now, just how in the hell did you think embarrassing me in front of everyone was helping?"

Her friend's normally jovial nature turned serious. "When you transferred to our school, you didn't know anyone. The same way I was at the start of the school year. I didn't want to be in the mean girl clique. Hell, I didn't want to be in any clique. But some of us aren't as good at being alone as you are."

"Trina, you know it's all good. After we kicked it in detention, we've been tight—"

"Nah, Shan, let me finish. From the moment I met you, it was clear you were smart. You were proud of your heritage, and I don't have any. I've always been able to blend in because I'm… well, I'm unnoticeable. You were born to stand out, but you choose to blend in. You're like a chameleon. I didn't understand it at first. I saw that the second day, you switched up your accent entirely. I didn't want you to make the mistake of thinking the girls I was hanging with were the crowd to fit into, 'cause they weren't. It was no fun over there, and I'm sorry how I handled it."

"You know, you could've saved yourself the ass whoopin' by telling me as much."

"Look, ain't nobody tell me you were Laila Ali. Where did you learn to fight like that, anyway?"

Shanice put the car back in drive and started heading towards the party. "After I lost my parents, I was always angry. It got to a point where I was just never afraid of pain, so fighting was my default. I'm learning to control it, for my sake, because I'm not always going to be the biggest person in the room, but I always want to be the toughest."

"Do you hear yourself, Shanice?"

"What?"

"What high schooler—hell, what person on Earth talks like that? *I have to learn to control myself*," Trina mocked. "This is why I tried to save you from The Mean Club. You're too smart and driven."

"I could handle myself."

"Oh, I know that now. What nobody knows is that your best talent is acting like you're not a threat when you're the most dangerous person in the room."

Present day.

Shanice woke up from another torrid bout of sleep as her body recovered from her near drowning. Her nausea had subsided, but her strength was nowhere near what it was the day before. She felt the effects of being waterlogged, compounded by the broken ribs and the drugs in her system.

That bitch tried to kill me.

Her ribs ached and her head was pounding. Still, none of that was a priority.

Her hand was still cuffed to the bedrail. She was being detained and wasn't sure why.

It wasn't long before her captor made his way into the room. For the first time, she was coherent enough to process what was happening.

A middle-aged white male in a red-and-black checkered flannel shirt walked in. He adjusted the red hunter's cap on his head and poured a glass of water.

Aw, shit. One of the good, ol' Virginia boys.

She looked over at him as he turned to her.

"You're gonna have to sit up to drink this," he said.

Shanice examined the man's soft green eyes and the length of his beard.

Yep, definitely one of these good ol' boys.

She sat up and sipped the water gingerly, her left arm pulling at the cuff. She softened her eyes and asked gently. "Mr... What's your name?"

"I'm Hal."

"Look, Hal, I'm not a threat to you. You can take these handcuffs off."

Shanice watched the man pace as he processed her words. After some consideration, he turned to her. "Respectfully, I don't know that. Hell, I don't know you, and the fact you just tried on your feminine charm makes me trust you even less. Do you even know how you got here?"

Shanice tried to remember. She had vague ideas on why she was so heavily drugged.

"That's what I figured. High on that stuff. Is that what you and that red-headed woman were fighting over? Drugs?"

"I was fighting? And what makes you think I was fighting over drugs?"

"Well, for starters, you were high as shit. Doesn't take this long to get over a little water in your system, and you sure as hell weren't sailing the ocean blue. You had your hands around that woman's throat before she knocked you off the boat."

"That was my boat! Look, Hal, I really need to get out of here. If you think I'm a threat, call the authorities. My name is Shanice Gibson. I'm a sergeant in the U.S. military. You can ask fo—"

"Where are you from?"

"Excuse me?"

"Earlier, when you were asleep, you were mumbling some gibber-ish, sounded like another language. Where are you from?"

Shanice dismissed the racial overtones of the question. "I'm from here. Look, Hal, I really just want these handcuffs off." She tried to lift the metal rail, waking the large labrador retriever, who until now had been hovering at the doorway.

Hal walked over and patted the dog on the head. "Down boy. Ms. Gibson, I'd stay calm if I were you. It's about Jordan's feeding time, and he loves dark meat. Now I'm gonna ask you again, where are you from?"

"I'm from Virginia. I went to Robert E Lee High. My name is Sergeant First Class Shanice Gibson. You can call the military base, they can validate my—"

"See, the thing is, when I saw your dog-tags, I called the military base to see if they knew who you were. They told me they never heard of ya. And then I get to lookin' on the back of your tags, and looks like there's a stained metal image of another flag on the back—"

"That's my homeland flag."

"But you just told me you were born here."

"Yes, I was born here, but I was raised—look, it's a complicated story, Hal. Just call the base. A man's life is in danger. I'll give you my commanding officer's direct number—"

"Lady, I don't trust a word coming out of that pretty little mouth of yours right now. If you were me, would you let loose a stranger claiming to be a military soldier with some funny markings on her dog-tags? Who was fighting in the middle of a storm? Would you let that person go?"

"Hal, you're being an asshole right now. Just call the army ba—"

Woof! Grrrr, the dog barked again at her tone. *Woof, woof.*

"Easy there, boy. I'm gonna do some diggin', Ms. Gibson, and if it all checks out, I'll gladly let you go."

Shanice struggled against the cuffs but it was pointless.

She glared at the man. "You do that, Hal, and if you don't mind, take your racist dog with you. If I'm gonna be a prisoner, at least let me sleep in peace."

Hal nodded and walked out the door.

She drank the water, assessing her options. There wasn't anything she could do right now, so she let the slumber take over.

3

JUNIOR YEAR

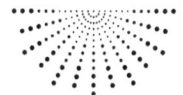

"**W**hat do you think?"

"I think this is amazing."

She watched Marcus as he smiled with pride at the mural on the side of the building. They were at the Fourth of July cookout at Virginia Beach.

He walked over and picked her up in one of his giant bear hugs she'd become accustomed to. When he put her down, he walked over to put a couple of final touches on what was a tribute to J. Cole, Virginia's very own.

The picture looked identical to the rapper. It impressed Shanice how Marcus had stuck with the painting. It was something he clearly had a talent for. She was excited to see her friend excited about something other than the snow cone shop and the military for once.

"I killed that shit, didn't I?" he asked enthusiastically.

"You did good, I can't lie."

"I already started on one just like this for the shop."

"Are you serious? Does the colonel know?"

"He's gonna have to visit the store to even see it. By that time, I'll be making money 'cause I've given it some much-needed flavor, and he's just gonna have to deal with it."

"You say that now, but I know you got a green Army jacket on standby."

"That's messed up. You don't have any faith in ya boy?"

"I have absolute faith in the fact that you're not gonna mess with your father like that."

The pair laughed as they walked down the beach.

Marcus grew quiet. She could tell he was deep in thought. As he kicked the sand with his sandals, he said, "Ms. Watson wants me to paint a picture of Michael Jackson on the back of her restaurant at the edge of the beach. Gonna pay good money, too."

He'd never asked for it, but she knew he needed her support and validation. "Marcus, that's incredible. You're gonna do it, right?"

"I mean, I want to, but... I don't know."

"What do you mean, you don't know?"

"I mean, when am I gonna do it, Gib? I've got school, taking Paul to all his lessons. I've gotta run the shop, and get my PT in so I can be ready for the physical at West Point. When am I gonna have time to—"

"Marcus, I know you're ready to go off and save the world, but don't think you owe it to yourself to discover what it would be like to be a kid for once?"

"And what does that mean?"

"It means, enjoy the moment. You're Paul's brother, not his guardian. That's not your responsibility, and as far as PT goes, you don't have to wake up at three in the morning to work out. You're supposed to be playing video games. You just painted a mural the entire school's gonna be talking about for the rest of the summer. Not to mention when they see what you do with Michael Jackson? I'm just saying, stop and smell the roses. Your murals have come so far since the 'LL Cool Jay-Z' debacle."

The pair chuckled, and she watched as Marcus pondered her words. "I don't know. My dad says artists don't make much money. He also says that the shop is a business move I'll appreciate when I'm older."

Shanice nodded in agreement, although she didn't really. Intuitively, she understood Marcus still idolized his father, that he was vested in pleasing his dad as best he could, but she also understood the young man who had become one of her closest friends. She'd be doing a disservice to the both of them if she didn't ask him. "Marcus, do you even want to go into the military?"

He looked at her, confused by the statement. "What does that even mean?"

"It means, do you, Marcus Winters Jr., want to join the military?"

There was a long silence. She studied his eyes, shifting away from her to process her words before he replied, "You know, it's been a long time since I've thought about anything else."

"A long time? Marcus, you're just a kid."

"Like I said, it's been a long time. Why are you even bringing this up?"

"Because I hear so much passion when you talk about these murals, and only expectation and responsibility when it comes to the military. I just think that whatever you're gonna do with your life, you should have that passion behind it."

"But my dad thinks—"

"Fuck what your dad thinks! What do *you* think?"

"Shanice—"

"You wanna know what I think? I think your dad puts too much pressure on you. It's one thing if you want to join the military, but if you're just doing it to fulfill your dad's expectation of you... well, that's no life at all."

"What would you know about parental expectations, Shanice? Your parents are dead."

Without thinking, she swung at him. He dodged her first punch, but her second one connected with his chin.

She swung a third time when he grabbed her hand.

"You asshole," she screamed angrily. She tried to hit him again, but he held her close.

"I'm sorry, Gib."

"Fuck you! Let me go!"

"Okay, I will, just don't punch me again, all right?"

Her fury subsided. She was still angry, but more hurt than anything.

She snatched her arm away from him and moved to sit on the beach, trying to suppress her tears. Her waves of emotion were just as furious as the waves crashing at her feet.

After a moment, Marcus came and sat next to her.

"I'm so—"

"Fuck you, Marcus."

"Okay, I deserve that. Listen, Gib, I know what I said was fucked up, it's just... when you brought up the military... I don't know, I mean, part of me has been wondering the same thing, and so I said something really stupid and insensitive, so I didn't have to think about what you said. I don't know how anyone knows how to be an adult, and I'll be honest with you: I'm scared, 'cause I feel like I should know by now. But look, my dad is a war hero. You've seen the way people act around him. It's a lot of pressure to live up to. I just... man, I'm so sorry."

She watched the waves crash while Marcus fiddled with his thumbs. Despite his outburst, she knew he didn't mean it.

"When I was living in Nevis, my aunt was my hero, because she was my dad's hero. Everyone talked about Theresa, how she traveled the world, and would send us gifts from everywhere. Now I know she hasn't gone anywhere, or done anything; she just has an Amazon account and a lot of credit card debt. But my dad made it seem like his sister had this amazing life. He was so proud of her, and *I* wanted to be the thing he was proudest of. I felt like if I traveled the world, maybe he'd be just as proud of me.

"The moment he was taken from me, I realized I could never make that happen. I had to come up with my own dreams. I still want to see the world, but I know, deep down, I want to stop the kind of people who killed my parents. I want to see the world, and eat exotic foods, but I'll give my life to hunt the kind of people who took everything from me, if only to stop them from doing it to someone else. That's my why. You have to figure out your why, Marcus. Not your dad's or anyone else's. What's your why?"

SHANICE WOKE up and looked around. She was alone.

"Hal?"

Still, no one came.

She screamed for help, to no avail.

She wrestled with the bed and noticed that a bolt was loose. She used her free hand to unscrew the bolt until the tips of her fingers bled.

"Almost there, Gib, push through it," she muttered.

Her wrist was bruising, and her fingers were bleeding, but she didn't stop until she heard the bolt drop to the floor.

"What's going on in there?"

She could hear the footsteps of her captor and his dog approach. Shanice looked at the frame that was almost loose. She was close, but for now she was out of time.

She laid back in the bed and, when he opened the door, she screamed, "Hal, you gotta let me go. You're scaring me."

"I'm not gonna harm ya, lady. I just need some answers."

"You've had plenty of time to call the police, Hal, which makes me wonder what you're really up to."

"Storm's been interfering with the signal—"

"You know, Hal, you've got all these questions about me, but I know very little about you. For starters, where are we, and why are you out here by yourself?"

"Just keep it down in here, will ya?"

Hal walked out of the room.

4

SENIOR YEAR

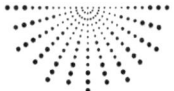

"'Yo, Marcus, lemme holla at you real quick.' No, that's too aggressive," she muttered to herself.

"'Look, Marcus, I know you and Bianca broke up, and I know you had your heart set on prom, so why don't we go together?' Ugh! That's too friendly. That's how you got in this mess in the first place!"

Shanice shook her head in disapproval. She was sitting outside the house waiting on him to go tuxedo shopping.

Working up the nerves to finally say how she'd been feeling over the years. "'Marcus... see, you're not going to prom with anyone, and well, neither am I, so maybe'... that's stupid."

She'd been working up the courage over the past few weeks to say something to him since school was about to end and everyone was going their separate ways. She wanted to at least let him know how she felt.

"'Marcus, we've been friends for a long time, but since the moment I laid eyes on you, I knew you were special to me. Ever since I met you, I've laughed more. I've learned more and I'm most comfortable when you're around. I can be myself with you, and I think you feel the same way. What if we found out what it would be like if we were together?'"

Tap, tap.

Marcus knocked on the passenger window, startling her.

She took a deep breath, composed herself, and muttered, "This is it, girl. You can do it."

She opened the door and Marcus sat down and slammed the door, rattling the little confidence she'd mustered.

"Sorry. I didn't mean to slam the door."

She could see he was upset. She wanted to ask what was wrong, but she knew if she didn't speak her truth now, she may never.

"Marcus, we've been friends for a long time—"

"You got a smudge on your head."

"I—what?"

"I think you have some motor oil on your forehead."

Shanice wiped the smudge from her forehead, adding to the collection of oil on her white muscle shirt.

She turned to see Marcus wiping tears from his face. "Marcus, what's wrong?"

Her friend was crying. He didn't even pretend to stop.

She knew he was hurt. It could only mean one thing.

"I didn't get into West Point."

She wanted to say something, but now wasn't the time for words. Her feelings would have to wait for another night.

She sat quietly next to her friend, who sobbed openly.

She held him as he leaned into her and groaned. "I tried so hard. I'm so stup—"

"Shhhh, you're not stupid, Marcus. You're one of the kindest people I know, with one of the biggest hearts."

"I just want him to be happy with me. He's never happy with me, Gib."

"I know. My aunt is just like that."

"How do you live with it?"

"With what?"

"Disappointing her all the time."

Shanice chuckled. "Well, for starters, I don't give a damn what she thinks. One thing I've come to realize about adults: people aren't who they say they are. We're all trying to be something else for someone else. Marcus, I asked you this a year ago, and I'll ask again: do you want to go to the military?"

"Are you kidding? It's all I've ever wanted."

"I'll ask you again. Do you, Marcus Bernard Winters Jr., want to go to the military?"

He pondered her words and, after a spell, looked into her eyes. "It's all I've ever known."

"And that's the problem, Marcus. There is such a big world out there that you're more than capable of taking on. It doesn't have to be in a U.S. Army uniform. You can—"

"That's easy for you to say, Shanice, you got into West Point."

"No, I didn't," she said blankly, startled by his statement.

Marcus, who also looked confused, wiped his eyes. "I don't under-stand. How are you going to the military?"

"Marcus, you know you don't have to go to West Point to be in the military, right?"

His shocked face revealed he did not, in fact, know this. He shook his head in disbelief. "Wait, you don't? But my dad always told me..."

Shanice closed her eyes, biting her tongue to hold in what she thought about his father, but she failed. "That's what I've been trying to tell you, Marcus. Your dad doesn't have all the answers. What do you think those recruiters were at school for?"

"My dad wouldn't let me talk to them. He told me they were the janitorial staff."

Shanice buried her face in her hands out of frustration. She then clasped her hands together. "Honestly, Marcus, you are so smart, but so stupid at times. Listen, even if you do get into the Army, you're gonna have to start thinking for yourself, because your dad won't be there to protect you. The real question is, do you want to go? Because I know you have a talent inside of you waiting to get out."

Marcus nodded. "You're right. My talent is to show the world what kind of leader a Winters is supposed to be. Shanice, you gotta get me to this recruiter's office."

"Marcus, I... please—"

"Shanice, if our friendship has ever meant anything to you, you'll take me to the recruiter's office. I have to do this."

He'd never forgive himself for not trying, she knew it. "I want you to know that I think it's a mistake. But it's yours to make. I'll take you."

"Thank you, Gib! Oh man, you don't know what this means to me. You've always found a way when there seems to be none."

Present day

When Hal walked into the room, Shanice stood in front of him

"Hi, Hal."

"What in the—"

Before he could reach for his pistol, Shanice charged him, sending both of them crashing into the dresser against the wall, glass spilling to the floor.

Shanice picked up a shard and stabbed Hal in the thigh, digging in hard.

As Hal screamed in pain, he grabbed her by the neck and pushed her all the way back onto the bed. He punched her in her broken ribs.

Shanice pushed through the pain and poked Hal in both eyes. He screamed in agony as Shanice slipped around him and put him in a choke hold.

Hal tried to apply pressure to her ribcage, but it was too late. Shanice had a firm grip around his windpipe. For a moment, she thought about killing him. But she knew the authorities needed to deal with Hal.

She searched for his gun after he'd passed out. As soon as she found it, she scrambled out of the room where she'd been confined. She entered the living room and found the main door double-bolted.

She took the gun and shot the lock off. She opened the door, stunned by what she saw on the other side.

"Oh, my god."

There was a room full of men looking at surveillance monitors of the room she was just in.

She cocked the pistol. "You got five seconds to tell me what in the hell is going on."

Some of the men grabbed their weapons. Shanice was about to shoot when a voice interrupted. "I'll take it from here, men. Stand down."

She couldn't place the voice initially, but as she turned around, nothing could have prepared her for who was standing in front of her.

"Director Caldwell?"

ENLISTMENT

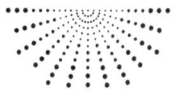

"'Welcome to the United States Army!' When he said that I almost fell over!" Marcus said as they walked into the snow cone shop. It was the third time he said the phrase, *I almost fell over*, Since they'd left the recruitment center.

Shanice smiled. She was happy for her friend. He'd never looked more excited. She asked a question she already knew the answer to. "How do you feel?"

Marcus paused to ponder her words.

"Honestly… I'm proud. And not because this is what my dad wanted. But at some point, I think this is what *I* wanted. What I dreamed about. And I got you to thank for that, Shanice."

"Marcus, you don't have to—"

"Wait, I want you to hear me. No one has ever cared about me the way you do. Not my mom, not dad. I know you're in my corner." He picked her up and held her in one of his giant bear hugs.

Shanice smiled like the schoolgirl she was. She'd been learning to accept they were friends, because he'd never seen her as anything more. She wanted that to change today.

Tell him you love him.

As he put her down, she looked in his eyes, full of hope and restoration.

She leaned in and wanted to kiss him, but first she needed to say what she'd been working on all day long.

She took a deep breath. "Marcus, we've been friends for a long time—"

"Shanice!"

A chill went up her spine as she instantly recognized the voice.

She looked over and saw her aunt Theresa, scowling at her.

Theresa snatched her away from Marcus and yelled, "So, this is what you do with your time, huh?"

"Yes, Auntie, I spend my afternoons hanging out at my old job. Bad stuff goes on here."

"Me nah study you, Shanice! Me bust my ass every day and me nah gonna feed another mouth. Ya hear me?"

"I'm not sure why that's a problem when you don't even feed this one."

Her aunt slapped her and screamed, "Get in the car."

Shanice looked at Marcus and handed him her keys. "Drive yourself home. I'll be by soon."

Shanice stormed off and got in her aunt's car. The drive home was miserable. Her aunt called her everything but a child of God as Shanice tried to block out her noise.

When they got home, Shanice walked into the room and looked around.

There's nothing for me here.

It was time to leave. She was already on her own. There was no sense in pretending otherwise. She was headed back to her room when her aunt stopped her.

"You'll sleep on the floor since you nah wanna respect for me."

Shanice started to pack her things.

"Chil', did you hear me? I said—"

"I'm not sleeping here at all."

"Excuse me?"

"Ever since I got to this country, you've been nothing but shit to

26

me. I pay half the bills, I bought my own bed, and I buy all the groceries, and you still think you get to be in charge? Fuck that."

Theresa tried to hit her but Shanice dodged her. "And that's another thing. I've sat here and let you beat on me for years, knowing I could've knocked your old ass out. But I'm not going to get hit by you again. The next time you raise your hand at me, be prepared to defend yourself." She shoved her aunt's hand back in the direction it came.

"You are the worst thing that ever happened to me, a little demon sent here to make my life a living hell! You are a bloody soucouyant!" Her aunt spat at her feet.

Shanice recalled the tales of the evil spirit in West Indian folklore, a demon who would disguise herself as a woman and steal the souls of the people around her. The Caribbean boogieman everyone was afraid of. The words would've hurt her to the core had she cared at all.

"I'm sorry you wish I'd never been born. But you won't have to worry about me ever again."

Shanice picked up her bag and walked out the door.

"Where are you going?"

"I'm going to disappear out of your life. I'm a soucouyant, remember?"

Shanice shoved her aunt out of the way and walked out of the house.

Present Day

"You can put the weapon down, Sergeant Gibson. You won't be needing it."

Shanice held the gun steady towards him.

The man behind all of this. Director Caldwell.

"I'm not going to put the weapon down until somebody tells me what the fuck is going on."

27

"Sergeant Gibson, the first thing you need to know about the CIA is that we don't negotiate. Either lower the weapon, or the red dots pointed at your torso, head, and heart will do it for you."

Director Caldwell raised his hand. Six infrared dots appeared on her body.

Realizing she was heavily outnumbered, she lowered her weapon.

Director Caldwell lowered his hand, and the men all lowered their weapons. Shanice watched as four of the six men left the room.

She turned to the director. "Hal, he's one of yours?"

"Yes, the man you refer to as Hal is one of ours. Six, go check on Agent Reynolds."

Shanice scoffed at learning that Hal wasn't his real name.

She looked to Caldwell. "So, this was all a test?"

"It was."

"I can't believe it. How did you know I was gonna get out of those handcuffs?"

"If a pair of handcuffs stopped any field agent for too long, they shouldn't be in the field."

Shanice watched as the last soldier in the room rushed over to assist in helping carry the man she'd come to know as Hal. She was remorseful now, knowing how close she was to killing him, but only a little.

She turned to Caldwell. "So, this… all of this, getting me here, locking me up, was it all a part of your extraction plan? How far back did it go?"

Caldwell removed his glasses and wiped them as he replied. "We had nothing to do with Corporal Holt and her plans for your demise, but we saw an opportunity to test you in a high stress environment while wounded. Realizing it was an ideal way to determine what kind of agent you'd be, we took advantage of it, and I have to say, you exceeded even our expectations."

Shanice flared at his response. "You sick mother— She could've killed me! I could've died."

"But did you die, Sergeant Gibson? I don't think you're under-standing the gravity of the job you're about to take on. Every hour of every moment of the rest of your life, someone will be trying to kill you. We deal in death so the rest of the world can live in peace. And for the record, you didn't die. We made sure of it. You're welcome." He replaced his glasses on his face.

Shanice wasn't happy about any of it. "So, did you arrest her?"

"And why would we do that?"

"Oh, I don't know, the attempted murder?"

"Sergeant, when the Agency disappears a person, we erase their school records, dental records, any kind of personal details that most people never think about. This isn't a straightforward task. Someone motivated enough could find a single shred of information, and that is how field agents get killed. But if a person with limited family is already presumed dead... Well, then, the search for you goes cold. In your case, the search would lead to your death at sea, the way the good corporal intended. If anyone looks hard enough, they'll find what Corporal Holt did and why."

"So, you're leaving this breadcrumb trail in case anyone looks for me?"

"It's the best way to protect you and those you care about."

"But I have evidence that she's—"

"We are well aware of what Corporal Holt is doing, and why, Sergeant Gibson."

His callousness shocked her. Frustrated, she replied, "Then you know that Marcus... Sergeant Winters, is really in danger."

"It would appear so. Now, are you ready to discuss our assignment?"

Caldwell's cold nature disturbed her as she realized she was the only person in the room who cared about Marcus.

She headed for the door but was stopped by a guard. "I have to go. I have to get back home."

Caldwell stepped in between her and the guard. "Sergeant Gibson, the United States government needs an operative *now*. I can guarantee you the inner workings of your interpersonal relationships were not on the CIA's priority list when they considered you as a candidate. You can decline this offer, but I can assure you there will never be another one. Now, are you ready to hear your mission briefing or not?"

Shanice thought about Caldwell's words and chuckled at the irony. The two things she'd fantasized about all her life were right in front of her, and she had to choose: telling Marcus Winters that she'd always loved him, and in turn saving his life, or being an operative for the CIA. An impossible choice between love or loyalty that she had to make now.

"She's killing him, Caldwell. I'm not sure if I could live with myself if something happened to him."

Caldwell waved to the guard to leave the room.

"This is the CIA, Sergeant Gibson. We have no qualms leaving a man behind. We have no family, no friends. We have only one objective: complete the mission. What we did with you was child's play compared to what you'll be doing in the field. So, let me offer you one last piece of earnest advice: if the burden of letting your childhood friend die knowing you could have saved his life weighs you down, this is definitely not the job for you."

Shanice stood there, bleeding, ribs broken, huffing heavily.

She locked eyes with Caldwell. Reflected in his was a roadmap. A man, once humane, now hollowed and hardened by the horrors he'd seen, and he was allowing her to see his entire truth. He'd pledged fidelity to the CIA decades ago, knowing he would die part of it. There would be no turning back, and there was no time for remorse.

As comprehension dawned, Shanice asked, "When do we start?"

SHANICE GIBSON's story continues in Code Name: Soucouyant

ABOUT THE AUTHOR

Norian Love is a best-selling author, screen-writer, songwriter, and poet, whose character-rich storytelling and creative world-building is swiftly setting him apart as one of the top writers in the black romance genre. His latest release, Autumn: A Love Story, was the recipient of the Association of Black Romance Writers 2021 Book of the Year Award. Autumn's complementary poetic journal, Blue: Love Letters to Fatima, also became a number one best-seller, giving him the unique distinction of having number one releases across multiple genres. He was a finalist for the 2021 Black Authors Rock, Author of the Year Award, as well as a finalist for the 2022 Romance Slam Jam Best Erotic Romance EMMA Award. He is working on completing the highly anticipated Money, Power, & Sex series and is currently serving as the head screenwriter for the University of Houston HIV Awareness campaign.

Penning the hashtag, #blacklovematters, Norian has been garnering accolades for his work from his reviewers, fans, peers, book clubs, and several podcasts. His books are sold worldwide and are published in print, eBook, and audio formats.

To learn more, visit www.norianlove.com or follow him across most social media outlets at @norianlove.

ALSO BY NORIAN LOVE

Novels

Money, Power & Sex: A Love Story

Seduction: A Money, Power & Sex Story

Donovan: A Money Power & Sex Novella

Autumn: A Love Story

Marcus: A Money, Power & Sex Novella

Poetry

Theater of Pain

Games of the Heart

The Dawn or the Dusk

Blue: Love Letters to Fatima

Music

Autumn: A Love Story: The Soundtrack

Coming Soon

Ronnie: A Money, Power & Sex Story

Code Name: Soucouyant

In the Case of Alexandria Hughes

www.ingramcontent.com/pod-product-compliance
Lightning Source LLC
Chambersburg PA
CBHW071237170626
46809CB00008BA/3103